**Take Care
of Yourself**

Staying Safe from
Injuries

by Mari Schuh

PEBBLE
a capstone imprint

Published by Pebble, an imprint of Capstone.
1710 Roe Crest Drive, North Mankato, Minnesota 56003
capstonepub.com

Library of Congress Cataloging-in-Publication Data is available on the Library of Congress website.
ISBN 9781663976796 (hardcover)
ISBN 9781666326758 (paperback)
ISBN 9781666326765 (ebook pdf)

Summary: Describes how to stay safe both indoors and outdoors. Essential safety tips involving helmets, sunscreen, fire, and more are provided along with important information on what to do in case of injury.

Image Credits
Capstone Studio: Karon Dubke, 8, 9, 11, 15; Getty Images: John D. Buffington, 18, Thomas Barwick, 10; Shutterstock: Anna Golant (design element) throughout, Anutr Yossundara, 5, Creativa Images, 14, Daniil Demin, 20, FOTOGRIN, 21, goodluz, cover, LightField Studios, 7, New Africa, 19, sirtravelalot, 13, Suzanne Tucker, 17

Editorial Credits
Editor: Erika L. Shores; Designer: Heidi Thompson; Media Researcher: Jo Miller; Production Specialist: Tori Abraham

All internet sites appearing in back matter were available and accurate when this book was sent to press.

Printed and bound in the USA. PO4608

Table of Contents

Words in **bold** are in the glossary.

Staying Safe

Everyone likes to have fun. But it's also important to be safe. Be aware of what is around you. Be mindful of what you are doing. When you are **prepared**, you can stay safe. You can keep yourself from being **injured**. And you can have lots of fun!

Take Your Time

Everyone gets busy! Remember to take your time doing things. You might get hurt if you rush. Don't run on ice or on wet areas. You might slip and fall. Walk slowly.

Take your time when you fill your backpack. Pack only the things you need. Make sure your backpack is not too heavy. Then you won't get hurt when you carry it.

On the Move

Stay safe when you travel. When you ride in a car, use a seat belt. When you ride the bus, sit in your seat. Wait for the bus to stop. Then you can stand up.

Pay **attention** when you cross the street. Stop walking. Look and listen for moving cars and other **traffic**. Look left. Then look right. Look left again. Cross the street when no cars are moving.

Play Time

It's fun to play! Make sure you have the equipment you need to be safe. A helmet protects your head. A mouth guard protects your teeth.

Warm up before you play. Swing your arms. Walk in one spot. Learn the rules of the game. When you're done playing, gently stretch your body. It feels good!

Cuts and Scrapes

Ouch! You might get a cut or scrape on your skin. You might get a bug bite. Clean your skin with soap and water. Let your skin dry. An adult can help.

Put **antibiotic ointment** on a clean bandage. Then put the bandage on the cut. This will keep the cut from getting **infected**. A **scab** might form over the cut. Don't pick it. It is helping your skin heal.

Staying Safe from Fire

Fire helps us cook. Fire keeps us warm. But fire can be dangerous. Stay away from matches, candles, and fireworks. Don't touch hot stoves. Ask an adult to help you in the kitchen.

Practice fire drills at home and school. Practice staying low to avoid smoke. Plan an **escape route**. You can go to a safe place outside. If there's a fire, call 9-1-1. Always tell an adult.

Being Safe Around Water

Splash, splash! You can learn to swim. Take swimming lessons. You will learn and have fun. Always swim with someone else. Never swim alone.

Be safe at the lake. Wear a life jacket. It helps you float. Wear it when you are in or near water. A life jacket helps keep you safe.

Fun in the Sun

Everyone loves sunshine. But too much sun can hurt your skin. You might get a **sunburn**. Put on sunscreen about 30 minutes before you go outside. After two hours, put on sunscreen again.

Protect your face and eyes. Wear
a hat and sunglasses. Take a sun break.
Find an area with shade. You can be
safe and have lots of fun!

Your Safety Gear

Safety gear is important. It can also be a fun way to show your style. Try this activity to make your gear your own.

What You Need:

- your safety gear, such as your bike helmet or sports helmet
- stickers
- colorful tape
- reflective tape

What You Do:

1. Add your favorite stickers to your gear. How many stickers will you add? Have fun with it!

2. Now add some colorful tape. This will make your gear look different than other gear. What colors will you use?

3. Add strips of reflective tape. This will help people see you better. This can make you safer while you play.

Glossary

antibiotic ointment (an-ti-bye-OT-ik OINT-muhnt)—a thick, often greasy substance that kills germs so hurt skin can heal

attention (uh-TEN-shuhn)—careful watching and listening

escape route (ih-SKAYP ROOT)—a way to leave a building in an emergency

infected (in-FEK-tid)—filled with germs or viruses

injured (IN-juhrd)—damaged or hurt

prepared (pree-PAIRD)—ready for something

scab (SKAB)—the hard covering that forms over a wound when it is healing

sunburn (SUHN-burn)—sore skin caused by staying in the sun too long

traffic (TRAF-ik)—cars, trucks, and buses that are moving on a road

Read More

Bellisario, Gina. *Personal Safety Mission!: How to Spot Danger.* Minneapolis: Lerner Publications, 2022.

MacReady, R.J. *Staying Safe Outside and Online.* New York: Cavendish Square Publishing, 2022.

Schuette, Sarah L. *Fire Safety.* North Mankato, MN: Pebble, 2020.

Internet Sites

Fire Safe Kids
firesafekids.org

KidsHealth: How to Be Safe When You're in the Sun
kidshealth.org/en/kids/summer-safety.html

Safe Kids Worldwide: Bike Safety
safekids.org/bike

Index

About the Author

Mari Schuh's love of reading began with cereal boxes at the kitchen table. Today, she is the author of hundreds of nonfiction books for beginning readers. Mari lives in the Midwest with her husband and their sassy house rabbit. Learn more about her at marischuh.com.